Mermaid Kingdom is published by Stone Arch Books
A Capstone Imprint
1710 Roe Crest Drive
North Mankato, Minnesota 56003
www.capstoneclassroom.com

Library of Congress Cataloging-in-Publication data is
available on the Library of Congress website.

ISBN: 978-1-4342-9695-5 (library binding)
ISBN: 978-1-4342-9699-3 (paperback)
ISBN: 978-1-4965-0189-9 (eBook PDF)

Summary: When Cora is selected to be part of the
mermaids' elusive Spirit Squad, she is beyond thrilled.
But her happiness quickly fades when Rachel isn't
picked. And when Cora finds out the reason why Rachel
wasn't picked, her spirit is crushed. Cora has a big
decision to make. A decision she never thought she'd
have to make.

Designer: Alison Thiele

Artistic Elements: Shutterstock

Printed in China.
042018   000312

Cora's Decision

by Janet Gurtler

illustrated by Katie Wood

STONE ARCH BOOKS
a capstone imprint

Mermaid Life

⭐ Mermaid Kingdom refers to all the kingdoms in the sea, including Neptunia, Caspian, Hercules, Titania, and Nessland. Each kingdom has a king and queen who live in a castle. Merpeople live in caves.

⭐ Mermaids get their legs on their thirteenth birthdays at the stroke of midnight. It's a celebration when the mermaid makes her first voyage onto land. After their thirteenth birthdays, mermaids can go on land for short periods of time but must be very careful.

⭐ If a mermaid goes on land before her thirteenth birthday, she will get her legs early and never get her tail back. She will lose all memories of being a mermaid and will be human forever.

⭐ Mermaids are able to stay on land with legs for no more than forty-eight hours. Any longer and they will not be able to get their tails back and will be human forever. They will lose all memories of being a mermaid.

⭐ If they fall in love, merpeople and humans can marry and have babies (with special permission from the king and queen of their kingdom). Their babies are half-human and half-merperson. However, this love must be the strongest love possible in order for it to be approved by the king and queen.

⭐ Half-human mermaids are able to go on land indefinitely and can change back to a mermaid anytime. However, they are not allowed to tell other humans about the mermaid world unless they have special permission from the king and queen.

Chapter One

It didn't matter how much fun summer break was. The first day back to school was always really exciting. Sure, I was nervous for school to start again. But I was more excited than nervous.

I couldn't wait to find out what teacher I would have. I was hoping that my best friends Rachel and Shyanna would be in the same class as me. I could survive without them, but it definitely wouldn't be as fun. When school started, I wouldn't have to babysit my sisters all day, which was a huge bonus.

Plus, this was a big year for me. It was the first year I'd be able to audition for the Neptunia Spirit Squad. The Spirit Squad is an important part of each kingdom. The team attends school and community events, bringing a fun dynamic through dancing, singing, and cheering. Once you are on the team, you are a part of it for life!

I'd dreamed about being on the team since I was a baby, when Mom would tell me stories about being on the team. These days, my mom was so busy with my sisters that sometimes it felt like she's forgotten about me. Being on the Spirit Squad would definitely make her notice me!

On the morning of the first day of school, my little sisters helped me decide what to wear. I couldn't decide which top screamed Spirit Squad Member. I narrowed it down to a new purple one and my favorite light blue one. When I came out of the bathroom in my new purple top, my sisters clapped and yelled. It was clearly the winner.

Sometimes I complained about how loud my sisters were, but I liked having them around when I needed a cheering section. They really could be sweet sometimes.

"Cora! Rachel and Shyanna are here," my mom called to me.

"Just in time," I said.

"Bye, Cora! Have fun! Good luck with your classes!" my mom shouted as she tucked Jewel under one arm and chased Pearl and Ruby down the hall. Sweet or not, those girls were a lot of work!

"Bye!" I called to my sisters and my mom, even though I knew they weren't listening.

"Wow!" Shyanna said. "That purple top really pops on you!"

"Thanks." We raved about each other's outfits. I admired Rachel's curly red hair and Shyanna's braids. The three of us linked arms and started swimming toward the school. Luckily I lived pretty close, which is why we all met up at my place.

"I'm really nervous," Rachel said as we approached the front of the school. I wasn't surprised that Rachel was nervous. She moved to Neptunia over the summer, and being the new girl was tough. Plus, it made me feel better that I wasn't the only nervous one.

"Don't worry, we've got your tail," Shyanna said.

"It's my legs I'm more worried about," Rachel joked, trying to relieve some tension.

Rachel was half-human, which was a big secret. She didn't want any of the kids to find out and bully her. She'd had some problems at her old school, so it made sense that she would hide her secret.

Shy and I were excited to catch up with our school friends and to introduce them to Rachel. We knew they were going to love her as much as we did. We reached the school and stopped to admire the giant statue of the school's founding mermaid, Michelle, at the school entrance. We showed Rachel how to rub Michelle's fin for luck.

"Everyone's going to love you just the way you are," I told her. I didn't think anyone would care that she was half-human, except maybe to think it was super cool that she could go on land whenever she wanted and for as long as she wanted.

We swam together through the pillars of old white coral that led into the school grounds. It was chaotic inside. Merboys and mergirls of all ages were doing flips and mingling and waving at each other.

"Hi!" I yelled to Cassie Shores as she swam by with a group of mergirls. She was one of the most popular mermaids at school and was also on the swim team with me last year. Like me, she was excited that this year we were eligible to try out for the Spirit Squad.

"She's a shoo-in for the Spirit Squad," I told Rachel. "She composes songs, and she's amazing at it. Making the Spirit Squad will be a great way for you to get to know her too!"

"Cool," Rachel said. "If you like her, so will I."

"She's as obsessed as Cora about being on the Spirit Squad," Shyanna said.

"I wouldn't say obsessed," Cora said.

"I would!" Shyanna winked to let me know it was okay, but Rachel wasn't paying attention. Instead, she was looking at a group of mermaids swimming by.

"That's the girl who said things about my mom during the Neptunia talent show," Rachel whispered to us.

"That's Regina," Shyanna said. "She's not the nicest mermaid."

"That is a huge understatement! She is just mean," I said as I glanced at Regina and frowned.

I needed to show positive behavior since the Spirit Squad selections were coming up, but it wasn't always easy.

Chapter Two

I didn't have long to dwell on Regina and her mean ways because Principal Tetra's voice boomed over the PA system. "Attention, everyone. Please report to the Dolphin Gymnasium. We are ready to announce class placements for this school year. Also, we have a special surprise this morning."

A special announcement? That sounded like a great way to start the school year!

We joined the crowd of merkids swimming into the gymnasium. Everyone was whispering and pointing, and I certainly understood why when I saw who was on the stage.

"That's the King and Queen!" Shyanna whispered, but it was pretty obvious. They were wearing crowns and were so regal looking with their shiny hair and sparkling tails. They were a beautiful couple!

Our principal stood on the stage. "Welcome back, everyone! Before the King and Queen make their special announcement, I am going to read the list of class assignments for the year. Please settle down and listen closely."

It took a couple of minutes to get all the merkids organized. Rachel, Shyanna, and I stuck together. Rachel was gripping our hands so tightly it hurt. She was also looking a little panicked. Since she was new at school, she was a little nervous about everything. I smiled to show her that we were all in this together.

As the principal read name after name, I was getting even more hopeful that the three of us would be in class together. And guess what? That's exactly what happened! Shyanna, Rachel, and I were in Ms. Swift's class list together!

Once the excitement of class assignments died down, Principal Tetra announced the King and Queen. The entire crowd went quiet as the pair stood and moved to the front of the stage.

"As you all know, this is the one-hundredth anniversary of Mermaid Kingdom," the King said. "To celebrate, there will be a Mermaid Kingdom Festival, including a special competition between individual kingdoms."

"Merkids from each kingdom will form teams to compete in a series of special spirit competitions, including singing, dancing, and chanting or cheering," the Queen announced. "We want to wish the merkids of Neptunia good luck!"

"The team that shows the best teamwork throughout the competition will win a trophy and a big donation for their kingdom and school," the King added.

A cheer rose from the merkids gathered in the gym. I couldn't believe this was happening! Since it was the one-hundredth anniversary of Mermaid Kingdom, being on the Spirit Squad was even more important than ever!

The Queen raised her hand again. "Earlier today, we picked the team leader for Neptunia. Based on community involvement and outstanding school achievements, Regina Merrick is your team leader."

As Regina, with a smug look on her face, confidently waved at everyone, there were polite claps. There were more groans than cheers.

I was really hoping Cassie would get to be the team leader, as she was nice, fair, and talented. There wasn't anything I could do about it now but politely clap and deal with it.

Principal Tetra congratulated Regina, thanked the Queen and King for their appearance, and dismissed us to our classrooms. The chaos and noise quickly returned as we swam out of the gym.

"Are you nervous about trying out for the Spirit Squad?" I asked Rachel.

She bit her lip and nodded. "I don't think Regina likes me very much."

"Regina doesn't like many people," Shyanna said.

"Don't worry about her!" I said with a smile. "With your voice, you're perfect for the team! You may be new, but you've already been noticed."

Shyanna looked at me and then back at Rachel. "Maybe Rachel doesn't want to be on the Neptunia Spirit Squad," she said.

"What? That's crazy!" I said. I couldn't even imagine not wanting to be on the team.

"That's not it. I'm just nervous," Rachel said.

"Me too!" I told her.

"I don't know why you're so nervous, Cora," Shyanna said. "You are super athletic and everyone likes you. Plus, you have a great attitude about everything, which is rare."

"Thank you, Shy," I said, blushing a little.

"You're perfect for the Neptunia team, just like your mom was," Shyanna said as she turned to Rachel. "Cora's mom was on the Neptunia Spirit Squad for the seventy-fifth anniversary of Mermaid Kingdom. She helped bring the trophy to Neptunia."

"I want to start practicing right away," I said. "Can we practice at your cave, Rachel? My sisters will be in the way at mine."

"Sure!" Rachel said. "Maybe my dad can even help us with a new song."

"Awesome! We really can't get better help than the music instructor for the Queen!" I said.

"See? Just because Regina is in charge doesn't mean we can't have fun, right?" Shyanna said.

I nodded, thankful. What would I do without my friends?

Chapter Three

By the end of the week, I was in full school mode. The school year was going pretty great. I loved Ms. Swift. We were studying shipwrecks in sea studies, and we even went on a field trip to explore an old sunken ship. Ms. Swift always let Rachel and Shyanna and me work together. The only thing that made my heart feel sad was that Rachel seemed so different at school. At school, Rachel was really quiet and reserved. Shyanna and I did everything we could to involve her, but it didn't help.

There was nothing wrong with being shy, but that wasn't the real Rachel. When she was with me and Shyanna alone, she was so full of spark and energy. But at school, she was so worried about the other mermaids finding out her secret that she barely talked at all. It made me sad. I could not imagine trying to be someone else all day just to fit in!

Rachel thought the merkids wouldn't want to be friends with her if they knew she was half-human. I knew Cassie and her group of friends would accept Rachel no matter what. They were cool girls. They knew what was really important in life.

I told Rachel she should be proud and announce it at the top of her lungs, but Shyanna explained to me that Rachel needed to do things her own way.

I had to stop focusing on Rachel and focus on tryouts for the Spirit Squad. My plan was to practice every day after school, but getting together with Shyanna and Rachel was harder than breaking open an oyster shell.

Because of the special anniversary this year, the tryouts were moved up and were less than a week away. They wanted to give the Spirit Squad more time to practice as a team.

Every time Rachel, Shyanna, and I scheduled an after-school practice, it seemed like there would be some sort of family emergency. First, Pearl got sick and I had to look after Jewel while my mom was at the doctor. Then, Jewel ripped her tail and needed stitches, so I had to babysit again. Just when everything seemed fine, Ruby got the flu and Mom made me stay home and help. Those three girls sure were a handful!

I often envied the quiet of being an only child, like Shyanna and Rachel. The two of them were getting in lots of practice time at Rachel's, and they didn't even need it.

I hated missing the practice time with the girls. I also hated missing out on the fun. Besides, Rachel's dad was the Queen's singing coach.

Fortunately, my sisters, my cousin Shelby, and my parents liked to watch me perform. They helped by singing Rachel and Shyanna's parts when I was practicing. I had my moves down, but I still wasn't confident about my singing. I knew Rachel and Shyanna would make the Spirit Squad because their voices were so amazing. My plan was to distract the judges from my singing voice by dancing my heart out. I could sing, but it wasn't my best talent. I could do decent harmonies, but I was no power singer like my friends.

But that wasn't going to stop me. I wasn't going to let anything stand in the way of making the Spirit Squad. I had been dreaming about this for too long to give up. All I could do was work hard and try my best. That had to count for something, right?

Chapter Four

Finally, the day for the tryouts arrived. Rachel, Shyanna, and I wore matching pink tops and pink nail polish. Shy's mom even made us matching braided sea flower tiaras.

Before our performance, the three of us put our heads together. "Let's do this, girls!" I told them. We swished our tails together, and then the music for our number started.

What happened next was kind of a blur. I know I hit all of my notes, and Shyanna and Rachel sang like angels. As for the dancing, we nailed it! We were in perfect unison, and each solo was unique and energetic. Afterward, I was so relieved to be done I could barely talk. We stayed to watch the other performers. I was impressed. Everyone did an incredible job, and with that kind of competition, I knew it was going to be tough to make the team.

When all the performers finished, Principal Tetra announced that the judges would go and vote. The judges were former members of the Spirit Squad. Since Regina was the team leader, she got to make all the final decisions.

I bit all the glittery nail polish off my nails waiting for the committee to return with the results. The water in the gym seemed electric, and everyone was bursting with excitement. Finally the committee members swam back inside, led by Regina. I felt positively seasick.

"Don't worry, Cora," Rachel whispered calmly. "You're going to make the team. I know it."

"The results are in," the principal announced. "Thank you to every mermaid and merboy who tried out for the Spirit Squad. You made the decision particularly difficult."

My breath was coming fast. Shyanna took my other hand as Regina stepped forward. She smiled with her pearly white teeth.

Rachel took a deep, nervous breath. It was my turn to squeeze her hand. "You were great," I whispered to her.

Rachel nodded, but her lips were one thin line again. She looked a little pale as well.

"With this being the one-hundredth anniversary of Mermaid Kingdom, you all know how important the squad is this year. Now I will hand things over to Regina for the big announcement," the principal said.

"Thank you. As mentioned, this year the Spirit Squad is more important than ever. The first member

member of the Neptunia Spirit Squad is . . ." Regina cleared her throat and paused.

"Cora Bass."

My entire body whooshed with relief. A grin took over my face. But then I looked beside me and my grin disappeared.

Rachel.

Rachel hadn't made the team.

Chapter Five

It didn't make sense. The judges hadn't chosen Rachel? But she was one of the best singers, not only in Neptunia, but in the entire Mermaid Kingdom. I couldn't believe she hadn't made the team!

"Don't be sad for me," Rachel said. "Go on up there and celebrate. You deserve this!"

She pushed me forward, cheering the entire time. When I got to the front, Shyanna tackled me with a giant hug. We did a somersault together and stopped at exactly the same time. When we looked out into the crowd at Rachel, she smiled brightly and gave us a big thumbs-up.

"I can't believe she didn't make it," I said to Shyanna.

"I know!" she answered. "It does not make sense. Something feels off about this entire process, and I bet Regina has something to do with it."

"I totally agree," Shyanna said, looking frustrated. "We need to get to the bottom of this, no matter what. Rachel does not deserve to be excluded."

The committee made some announcements, and then it was done. We swam back to Rachel.

"Don't feel bad for me," she told us as soon as we reached her. "I'm okay. I'm more than happy to help coach you two. I'm pretty good at coaching from watching my dad teach."

"Rachel, I have no idea why you aren't on the team," I said.

"But don't worry," Shyanna said. "We will figure it out."

We pulled her in for a group hug. When we let go, she blinked fast and smiled, but I saw a lone tear escape from her eye.

* * *

"That was a really great practice," Cassie said to me and Shyanna. It was fun spending more time with Cassie again. She was just as smart, funny, and kind as I remembered.

"Well, except when Regina said she had to leave early," Shyanna said, "and you offered to take over the practice. I thought she was going to have a temper tantrum, but you still insisted. I couldn't believe you did that."

I grinned. Shyanna didn't like conflict. As a big sister, I had lots of experience with it. "Nah. She was fine."

Cassie laughed. "Only because you didn't really give her a choice."

I shrugged. Regina could be mean sometimes,

but I didn't let her get to me. She was just another mermaid. I didn't have time to worry about her.

"You did a really great job leading our group," Shy said.

"I guess being bossy comes naturally to me," I said.

Shyanna shook her head. "No. It's not being bossy. It's being a good leader. After Regina left and you took over, we were a completely different squad. We worked together so much better, which is what we need to do to win this thing."

"You're good at motivating, which is a big role for the team leader," Cassie chimed in.

"Thanks," I said, blushing. "Regina is a really good dancer and singer, though."

"But she isn't a very good leader," Shyanna replied, making a good point.

"She tries," I said. I didn't want to talk about it anymore, even though I kind of agreed with her that Regina wasn't always the best at leading the group.

I didn't want to admit it to anyone, even Shy, but I'd lost some of my excitement about being on the Spirit Squad.

The fact that Rachel hadn't been selected still bothered me. Not just because she was a great friend — fair was fair — but because she was a great performer. I suspected that Regina maybe did have something against Rachel, and I needed to get to the bottom of it.

"Hey," I said. "My mom isn't expecting me to be home to babysit for another hour. Let's go to Rachel's and see how she's doing. We've been so busy with Spirit Squad lately that we haven't seen much of her."

"That's a great idea," Shyanna said.

"This is my cue to head home," Cassie said.

"Are you sure?" I asked. "You are more than welcome to come with us."

"I don't think Rachel would like that very much. I get it, though," she said. "Being the new girl is tough."

"Some other time," Shyanna agreed.

We each gave Cassie a hug and swam fast to see Rachel, swirling with excitement as we made our way over to Rachel's cave in the new part of Neptunia.

We swam up to the front door and rang the bell, but no one answered. We looked at each other.

"She's not home," I said.

"I wonder where she went," Shyanna said.

"She's probably helping her dad. Let's wait. I bet they'll be home soon," I said, hoping I was right.

We played with some sea turtles and chased after some cute baby crabs who were playing hide-and-seek. Finally, Rachel swam into view.

"There you are! Finally!" Shyanna said. "Where's your dad?"

"My dad?" she said.

"Weren't you helping him?" Shy asked.

Rachel smiled. "No. He's with the Queen. She's working on a new performance and needed his help."

Shyanna and I exchanged a quick glance as we followed Rachel into her cave.

"So where were you?" I asked, even though I could guess.

"I went to visit Owen." She swam over and stretched out on a hammock, looking very pleased with herself.

Owen was Rachel's best friend, a human she'd met on land. He'd recently been granted magical merman powers to visit us in Mermaid Kingdom for two hours at a time, but it was easier for Rachel to visit him on land.

Shyanna and I looked at each other again, and her worried expression echoed how I felt. Not so long ago, Rachel had been thinking about leaving Mermaid Kingdom to become human. What if she still wanted to?

"Why don't you bring him here?" I asked Rachel.

"I would rather go on land," she said and got up from the hammock. "Legs are restricting in the water, but they're kind of fun on land. I'm learning how to run faster. It's pretty amazing."

"You're sure you're okay?" I asked again. "You're not thinking about becoming human again, are you?"

Rachel shook her head. "Don't look so worried, you two. I'm fine. Really."

"We're your best friends," I said. "You can tell us anything."

"Well," she finally said, "maybe I feel a little left out because you two are so busy after school with practice. But it's okay. I don't want you to feel bad. I want you to do great at the Spirit Games."

We swam over and hugged her tight.

When we let go, she sniffled. "Maybe I'm a little scared you two are going to forget about me and things will be like they were in Caspian. I was so lonely there, and people made fun of me for being half-human. It was terrible."

"That's when you started hanging out with Owen, right?" Shy asked.

"Yes," Rachel said. "I don't know what I would have done without him."

"I hate that the Spirit Squad is making you feel so bad," I said. "It's supposed to make everyone happy, and I don't want to be a part of something that makes you miserable."

"I agree," Shyanna said. "We don't need to be a part of the Spirit Squad."

Rachel shook her head hard. "No. No way. I know how important this is to you two — especially you, Cora. I'm not letting you quit because of me. I'm fine."

"It *was* important to me, but our friendship is way more important," I said. "Besides, we don't have practice tomorrow, so we definitely need to hang out."

My phone rang then. It was my mom, telling me to come home. "We'll see you after school tomorrow, okay?" I told Rachel.

She smiled and nodded, but the smile didn't reach her eyes. That didn't make me feel any better.

I had to fix it. I just wasn't sure how.

Chapter Six

Before school the next day, Regina called a special meeting for the Spirit Squad. "The first competition will take place in ten days," she announced. "The contest will be at Caspian Castle, during the senior swim competition. Spirit Squads will perform between races. We need to win this and get off to a good start."

Everyone cheered and clapped.

"In preparation, we're going to have a special rehearsal after school today," Regina said.

My mouth dropped open. We'd promised Rachel we would be free to see her, but we really couldn't skip practice. Shy and I swam to find her and tell her the bad news.

"It's okay," Rachel said, smiling. "Don't look so guilty. It's exciting. I can't wait for the competition!"

The school day zipped past, and then the Spirit Squad gathered in the gym for our rehearsal. We lined up and started the routine.

My flips had really improved, and everything was going great, until the last part of the mermaid song. I opened my mouth to sing, but instead of a clear note, a horrible screech came out. It was so off key that everyone turned and looked at me. The music stopped playing. My face burned, and I covered my mouth with my hand. Regina put her hands on her hips and narrowed her eyes.

"Cora, what is wrong with you?" she said.

Everyone stared. My cheeks burned with humiliation, and my eyes filled with tears.

Shyanna swam close and patted my shoulder. "Don't worry about it. Just practice that note at home," she whispered. "You'll get it right."

We started again from the top. I fumbled through the song, singing really softly in case my voice cracked again. Regina did not look happy.

Shyanna and I swam home together, but after she left me to swim to her own cave, Regina swam up beside me. She must have been following us.

"Cora, you're the weakest link on our team," she told me. "We don't want to lose because of you. If you don't think you can hit that note properly, it would be better for everyone if you dropped out now."

I didn't want to let everyone down with my voice, but I wanted to be on the Spirit Squad more than anything. I shook my head.

"I won't mess up," I told her.

She glared at me and then nodded. "Please don't. We're having a full dress rehearsal tomorrow. You had better prove that you can do it."

With a flick of her tail, she swam away. I went inside my cave and immediately got swarmed by my sisters, who were arguing over a necklace of woven seaweed. I tried to shake off my gloom, but the tears came hard and fast.

Mom came into the room and swam to me. "Cora? Is everything okay?" She touched my forehead to see if I was warm. I wanted to tell her why I was upset, but she had enough to deal with all of my little sisters. I also didn't want her to know that the Spirit Squad wasn't perfect.

Just then, the doorbell rang.

"I'm fine, Mom. I'm just tired," I said. I fake smiled and went to answer the door. It was Rachel!

"You hang out with your friend," Mom said to me. "I've got the girls."

Rachel and I swam to my room. "Are you okay?" she asked. "I was coming home from visiting Owen and I saw you and Regina talking. It didn't look like a pleasant conversation."

I told her what Regina had said.

Rachel looked really mad. "Don't worry, Cora," she said. "I've got something that will help you."

Rachel asked my mom if I could go home with her. Mom let me go without even thinking about it. She knew something was wrong.

At her cave, Rachel dragged me inside her dad's room, which seemed really weird.

"Are we supposed to be in here?" I asked.

"It's okay. My dad keeps something of mine in his closet, but I'm allowed to take it out or use it anytime I want," Rachel said confidently.

She swam to the closet, but I floated by the doorway. Rachel took something out and turned, hiding it behind her back. She smiled. "You're not allowed to say no."

Then she pulled out the most beautiful mermaid top I'd ever seen. It sparkled with every color under the ocean with a shimmery, magical quality. It literally took my breath away.

"I want you to wear this. It was my mom's. The Queen gave it to her as a special gift when she married my dad. It's magical."

"Really?" I said, not fully believing her. "I think I need more than magic to help me be a better singer."

"Well, it helped my mom sing as charmingly and skillfully as a full-fledged mermaid," Rachel said. "Don't you think some magic had to be involved? She was a human!"

I stared at the shell top, completely amazed by how beautiful it was. Maybe it was magic!

"Oh, Rachel," I said, almost in shock. "I can't wear that. I'd be scared I'd ruin it or something. It's too much."

Rachel shook her head. "You are one of the most kind and responsible mermaids I've ever known. And you and Shyanna have made my life in Neptunia incredibly wonderful. I insist that you borrow it. I have complete trust in you. The magic will give you courage to perform as well as I know you can.

You only have to believe in yourself, as much as you believe in everyone else around you."

I didn't even know what to say. Rachel was amazing! She was willing to help me and our team even though Regina hadn't picked her.

Rachel held out the top and slipped out of the room so I could try it on. When I swam out wearing it, Rachel clapped and whistled.

"Wow!" Rachel said with a huge smile on her face. "It's perfect on you. I mean it! It was meant to be worn by you. My dad will be so proud to see you perform with it on."

"Are you sure?" I asked. I loved the top. Just the thought of wearing it made me believe I could sing better. "I feel so bad, Rachel. You're a gifted singer. You should be on the Spirit Squad. Not me."

Rachel shook her head. "No, really. Your voice is great, Cora. You only have to believe in it. Besides, you have much more than a voice. Your incredible spirit shines from you all the time. It makes you the wonderful mermaid you are. It sounds cheesy, but I look up to you."

Tears slipped down my cheeks, but they were tears of happiness. I changed out of the top and held it out to Rachel. "Take it with you," she said.

"On no," I told her. "I can't keep it at my cave. I'm afraid with all the chaos and my sisters around, it might accidentally get wrecked. I need all the help and magic I can get!"

She laughed, but took it back and hung it in her dad's closet. "I'll bring it to school tomorrow so you can wear it for your dress rehearsal."

I hugged her on my way out of her cave. "You are such a good friend," I told her.

"So are you," she said. "See you tomorrow!"

I swam home with an extra flick in my tail and a huge smile on my face. With that extra bit of magic, I had all the confidence in the world!

Chapter Seven

The next day at school, I put on the top before rehearsal. Rachel swam to the door of the gymnasium and peeked inside to watch the others' reaction. The other merkids were thrilled. They immediately surrounded me and raved about the shimmery, magical top. Even Regina swam over and nodded her approval, but she swam away quickly.

After the fussing was over, we ran through the singing number and my voice held the notes perfectly. The top really was magical!

When the rehearsal finished, I changed into my regular top. Then I told Shyanna I had to take the special one straight to Rachel. Shy said she'd come with me.

Rachel's dad greeted us at the door and smiled when I gushed about the magical top. "You would make my wife proud," he said, smiling. "Rachel's in her room."

I wanted to surprise Rachel, so I lifted my finger to my lips to tell Shy to be quiet. We quietly swam around the corner to her room and spotted Rachel on her bed. She was lying down with her head on her pillow, and she was weeping as if her heart was breaking into two.

Shyanna and I stopped. Rachel must have sensed us because she looked up. She immediately sat up straight, sniffled, and wiped her tears away.

"Hi, guys," she said, trying to sound cheerful. "What are you doing here? I think there's something in my eye."

"What's wrong, Rachel?" Shyanna asked.

We both swam to Rachel's bed and floated gently down beside her.

"What is it?" I asked.

"It's nothing. Nothing. How did they like the shell top?" she asked.

I crossed my arms. "You know they loved it. But we are not going to pretend that nothing is wrong. You're upset. And I think I know why."

Rachel's chin dropped, and she wouldn't look at Shyanna or me.

"It's Regina, isn't it?" I asked. "What did she do?"

"I don't want to ruin your happiness," Rachel said and her bottom lip quivered.

"We're best friends," I said. "If something is making you unhappy, we have to do something about it. After all, I certainly don't want to hear more talk of you going off to live as a human again. That was just crazy talk."

"Spill," Shyanna told her.

Rachel swallowed and looked at me. Then she lowered her eyes.

"Rachel," I said. "Please tell us."

"Regina saw me watching the dress rehearsal," Rachel whispered. "She told me to leave. She told me half-humans couldn't represent a mermaid kingdom, and she didn't want me ruining her practice."

My mouth dropped wide open. I glanced at Shyanna, who looked shocked too.

"She actually said that?" I asked.

Rachel nodded. She looked miserable.

"I'm quitting the Spirit Squad," Shyanna said. "If that is how the leader is treating merpeople, I don't want any part of it."

"Me too," I said as my heart twisted. It hurt to think about not competing, but it wasn't worth all of this unhappiness. "Happiness and friendship are what being a mermaid is all about," I told Rachel. "Not meanness or discrimination. Nobody should have to deal with that."

"You can't quit," Rachel insisted. "It's okay. I'm fine. Maybe I took it wrong. I'm just feeling sorry for myself. It doesn't mean you two are going to give up your dream."

Shyanna looked at me. We both knew it was more my dream than hers. But I shook my head.

"No. What Regina said is not okay. It's not okay. I can't believe the others feel this way too."

"Neither can I," Shyanna said.

I jumped up with a new determination. "I can't let this happen. I need to figure things out."

"Cora?" Shy called and swam quickly after me.

"It's okay," I whispered to her. "You stay here with Rachel. She needs one of us. I'm going to have a special meeting with Cassie. If anyone can help with this, she can."

Shy nodded. "Okay," she said. "Good luck."

Chapter Eight

I swam straight to Cassie's cave. She answered the door.

"Why didn't Rachel Marlin make the Spirit Squad?" I asked, not wasting any time.

Cassie glanced around the kitchen, looking really uncomfortable. "I guess some of the other merkids didn't think she was good enough for the team?"

I pressed my lips tight and spoke slowly, trying not to be too angry at Cassie. "Are you aware of how talented Rachel is?"

Cassie sat down across from me, wrapping her long blond hair around her finger, and avoided looking at me. "I know. Trust me, I wanted to have her on the team. I was outvoted."

"By Regina?" I asked.

"I don't think I'm supposed to say," she said.

"Well," I said angrily, "tell me this. Is it because Rachel's mom was human?"

Cassie's cheeks turned bright red. "I don't know, Cora. She didn't come right out and say that."

"What other reason could there be? She's got a great voice and great attitude. Plus, she's a great mermaid," I said.

Cassie sighed and shrugged. "I think maybe you should talk to Regina," she said. "There's not much I can do." She blinked at me with wide eyes, and I saw the sympathy in them. As if she wanted to help.

"Could you arrange a meeting for the whole Spirit Squad right away?" I asked. I wasn't going to let it go. I couldn't ignore it.

Cassie swam up. "Regina isn't going to be happy, but I'll see what I can do," she said.

* * *

Within an hour, Cassie had managed to get everyone over to her cave.

"I've called a special meeting," I said to everyone gathered in Cassie's kitchen.

Regina swam to my side. "I'm not sure why you're calling a special meeting when you're clearly not the team leader," she said.

Cassie swam to my other side. "Let her speak, Regina." She glanced out to the Spirit Squad. "Raise your hand if you want to hear what Cora has to say."

Shyanna's hand shot up first. Slowly, other hands went up in the air. It wasn't everyone, but it was enough for me to continue.

"I don't think I need to remind you that we are a team," I said. "The qualities we are trying to display are pride and joy for the Mermaid Kingdom."

The merkids around the kitchen nodded and a couple even whistled their approval.

"We're competing against the best singers and dancers and performers in the entire Mermaid Kingdom," I went on. "And we should have the most spirited merpeople representing us."

"We all know that, Cora," Regina said, rolling her eyes. "That's why we picked everyone here. And that's why I've been nagging you about your performance. We want to win."

"Exactly," I said. "And if we really want to win, we need Rachel Marlin on our team. She has one of the best voices in the entire kingdom, and she lives here in Neptunia. I'd like to know why she wasn't selected to be on our team in the first place."

The room was totally silent for a moment.

"Her voice isn't the problem," one of the mergirls blurted out. Everyone looked at her, and her cheeks went as red as lobster tails. She glanced at Regina with fear in her eyes.

"What exactly is the problem, then?" I asked, staring directly at Regina.

"Oh, come on." Regina rolled her eyes again. "She's — well, she's different."

"We're all different," Shyanna said. She swam to the front and floated close to me.

"Rachel is half-human," Regina said. "No one else is different like that."

"So Rachel really was excluded from the Spirit Squad because she's half-human?" Shyanna asked.

No one was brave enough to say anything or stand up to Regina.

"Why would that even matter?" I asked.

I didn't want to believe Rachel had been right. But no one was denying it.

I looked around the room. "I'm so ashamed," I told them. "This is no way to treat anyone."

"Well, if that's the way you feel . . ." Regina held out her hand and studied the glitter on her nails.

"You bet that's the way I feel," I said.

"Me too," Shy said. "Come on, Cora. Let's go."

We swam out of there together.

"I can't believe everyone in our school feels this way. It's just not right," Shyanna said sadly as we swam away.

"I don't believe everyone does. We have to go to the Queen," I told her. "We have to talk to her. This isn't right."

Chapter Nine

Even though we showed up at the castle unannounced, the Queen agreed to see us right away when we told her guard it was about the Neptunia Spirit Squad.

We told her the whole story. "And that's why we decided to come to you," Shy finished.

"Oh dear," said the Queen. "Rachel is such a lovely mergirl. And a beautiful singer too. You three did such a great job at my concert and at the talent show. I wondered why she wasn't selected to represent our castle. Her father must be upset."

"I don't think he knows yet," I told the Queen.

She tapped her finger on her chin, thinking.

"Well," she finally said. "I can't force the team to add Rachel." She smiled. "But there may be another solution." She paused for effect. "You could form a new group."

Shyanna and I looked at each other. "A new group?" I repeated.

The Queen nodded. "Each castle is allowed to enter more than one team. We never have before because we're one of the smaller castles. But . . ." She tilted her head slightly. "It can be done."

Shyanna and I smiled at each other. That just might work!

"We could recruit all the merkids in Neptunia who wanted to be on the Spirit Squad, but who didn't make it or were afraid to try out because of Regina," Shyanna said.

I nodded my agreement. "We could do it!"

"It sounds like a good idea," the Queen said. "A Spirit Squad that won't exclude anyone." She lifted a finger in the air. "I hereby appoint Cora Bass as the team leader for Spirit Squad 2."

"This is amazing!" I yelled.

The Queen smiled. "Okay, off with you two." She spoke in her more regal voice. "You have work to do. And it's time for my diving lessons."

We swam up, thanking her for her time and her great idea. She waved her hand in the air and another mermaid appeared. We both immediately recognized her. The swimming instructor was the Sea Olympic Champion, Sydney Lincoln!

"Oh, and girls?" the Queen called as we swam down the Royal Hallway.

We both turned back.

"Make us proud!"

Shyanna and I swam away and didn't say another word until we were outside the castle. We both stopped at the same time, let out big breaths, and started to giggle uncontrollably.

Just as quickly as I started laughing, I stopped. "Oh my goodness." I put my hand on my chest. "What did we just agree to? Can we even do this in such a short time?"

"I don't know," Shyanna said. "But we have to go tell Rachel the news."

We swam as fast as we could back toward Rachel's cave. "We have some quick recruiting and lots of practicing to do," I added as we raced to her neighborhood. "And I have to call my mom and see if she'll even give me permission to do this."

"You know she will," Shyanna said.

"I don't know," I replied, suddenly worried. "My sisters are a handful, and she needs my help a lot. I hope she understands."

"When she hears the whole story, she'll understand how important it is," Shyanna said. "You know your mom will support you."

* * *

When we got to Rachel's cave, Mr. Marlin answered the door. Shyanna spilled the news, including an exact playback of our conversation with the Queen.

"She's a great Queen," he said, and then the grin on his face stretched wide. "And Rachel deserves to be on a Spirit Squad. You girls are such good friends, and I am so happy she has you."

"Rachel!" we all yelled. "We have work to do!"

Rachel was thrilled about the new group. Her dad even offered to help coach us once we got more people together.

Shy and I called our mothers, and as Shy predicted, my mom was more than happy to give me the night off from babysitting for emergency recruitment for the new Spirit Squad. She said she'd manage without me as long as I needed to make my new group work. I heard the pride in her voice, and my heart swelled.

Shyanna's mom was happy too, and promised to make our entire group matching seashell headbands.

"By the way," Rachel told me, "that top you borrowed isn't magic. The magic comes from believing in yourself. Your singing was all you."

"No way!" I said. "You are pretty sneaky, Rachel."

"Magic or not, we have lots of work to do," Shyanna said. "Let's get started!"

We sat down and came up with a list of everyone who had tried out for the Spirit Squad but hadn't made it. We added a few names of merkids who we knew would love to be on the team, but were afraid of Regina.

Once we had our list, we swam through the entire castle, going door to door to personally ask the mermaids and merboys on our list if they wanted to join our group.

"It's going to be lots of work," we warned each of them. "We'll have to put in extra hours to be ready in time for the swim meet. We only have a few days."

Some mermaids and merboys didn't want to do it. But many did. By the end of the night, we had an enthusiastic and complete team. As team leader, I had to figure out what to do with them in a very short time.

It was up to me. I wondered if I could handle it.

Chapter Ten

Regina laughed when we told her we were resigning from her team and starting a new Spirit Squad.

"I have the entire gymnasium booked," she said with a toss of her hair. "I can't afford to share it. You'll have to find somewhere else to practice."

"No problem," Rachel told her. "We don't need it."

The team agreed to meet at Walrus Waterpark after school to practice. Our first practice proved we had a team with a lot of heart and oodles of spirit.

Everyone was focused and willing to work hard to learn a routine in a short time. The only trouble was, I couldn't get everyone to agree to sing the song I'd chosen. I knew it was a hard song, but it was one of my favorites.

Instead of wasting time arguing about it, we agreed to work on the dance routine while we thought the song over.

I showed everyone the choreography I'd come up with. Together we adjusted the moves to fit the skills and limitations of our team members. We all worked together, improvising and improving the moves.

The results were astonishing. It was obvious the dance routine was going to be our biggest strength as a team. All the merkids worked together. Our willingness to help each other shine and show off our differences was a definite advantage. We left our first practice with a solid routine that everyone loved.

Shyanna, Rachel, and I left together. As soon as we were out of the park, I burst into tears.

"Cora? What's wrong?" Shyanna asked.

"I'm happy, tired, and a little stressed," I said as I cried like a little baby. "I can't even get everyone to agree on a song, and we only have three days left to learn everything."

Rachel swam in front of me. "Don't be silly, Cora. You put together the most amazing routine I've ever seen. You had everyone taking ownership and working together. You were great."

"I'd like to help," a soft voice said.

I sniffled and looked up. It was Cassie Shore.

"I quit the Neptunia Spirit Squad." She looked at Rachel. "I knew it was wrong — why you didn't make the team. I'm sorry I didn't stick up for you sooner. I think it's awesome that you're half-human."

"It's okay," Rachel said quietly. "And I appreciate you saying that."

Cassie nodded. "I'm on your side."

Rachel smiled. "There shouldn't be any sides. We're all merpeople."

Cassie turned to me. "I saw you practicing, and I couldn't help noticing that you were having trouble with your song. I would love to help."

"That's right! You're a songwriter!" I shouted.

Cassie nodded.

"On one condition," I said. "I think our group will do better if Rachel is our team leader. Can you work with her to rewrite the song and help her teach it to the rest of the group?"

Rachel gasped. "Really, Cora? You want me to be team leader?"

"You're the best singer," I said. I glanced at Shyanna. "Well, you and Shy."

Shy laughed. "It's okay. Rachel is good. And she's much better at performing than I am. It's a great choice, Cora!"

The four of us put our hands out and piled them on top of one another in a perfect team huddle.

"We still have lots of work to do," I said. "But I'm glad we're all doing it together."

Chapter Eleven

"Mermen and mermaids, merboys and mergirls, welcome to the Mermaid Kingdom Festival to celebrate our one-hundredth anniversary," yelled the King of Caspian Castle. "First to compete, from Neptunia Castle, Spirit Squad 2!"

The crowd cheered. I glanced at Shyanna. She looked like she was about to be sick. Stage fright was hard for her.

"It's okay, Shy. You're far from alone. And you always do great," I whispered.

She nodded, took a big breath, and swam out into the giant field we would be performing in. From the opposite end of the field, Rachel swam to meet her in the middle. As rehearsed, we were all quiet and still, and then the two of them opened their mouths and started to sing.

The rest of the team swam in fast, doing flips over each other like a giant game of leapfrog. Then Rachel rolled out a big ball of glowing plankton that went off like fireworks. The effects were amazing, and the crowd roared with approval.

The whole team started singing the song that Cassie had composed and Rachel had taught us, and we moved together in a giant wave of motion. We had even added special effects to our routine by using lots of glowing creatures.

There were a few mistakes in our performance here and there, but the crowd was cheering so loudly that I don't think anyone noticed the glitches. I could not believe it was happening.

The finale came quickly, and we all worked together and jumped and sprang off each other like we rehearsed. The final roar of our team could be heard throughout the entire kingdom. "Neptunia!" we shouted as one.

After the crowd settled down, the swim meet got underway. There would be a few more events, and then the other Spirit Squads would perform their routines. I was excited to see what the other groups had put together.

Our team huddled together once we swam off the field. "I'm so proud of every single one of you!" Rachel said. "No matter what happens!"

Merpeople from every castle flocked over to congratulate us. Regina swam by, her nose in the air. "I noticed so many errors in that first performance. How embarrassing," she said to her new co-captain, loud enough for us to hear.

"Yeah, but the performance was pretty spectacular," the co-captain said. "All those special effects and moves were ambitious for a group that just got together. And those mermaids can really sing!"

Rachel giggled. "She won't be co-captain long," she whispered to me.

Our entire team was sitting together when they announced the winner. It was the team from Hercules Castle. Their routine had been the best.

Shyanna swam over to us then. "Rachel! Guess who showed up to surprise you? He was in the crowd and saw our performance."

"Owen's here?" Rachel asked, grinning.

"He didn't know what time we performed so he got here early. He's only got his tail for another hour, so come on." Shy grabbed Rachel's arm. "Come on, Cora!" she shouted to me.

"I'll be there in a minute. I have to find my family!" I called and waved them off.

Everyone around me was gone, and I closed my eyes and took a deep breath to enjoy the moment.

The pace had been crazy over the last few days, but it had been worth it. Our performance was over, and we'd done really well.

When I opened my eyes, my mom was swimming toward me. She was alone, which truly never happened. "Where are the girls?" I asked.

She smiled. "Your sisters are with your father. He needs some practice handling all of them at once. He took some time off of work so I could come and see you." She winked and floated to my side. "That was an amazing show!"

I put my head on her shoulder, enjoying having her all to myself. "Thanks, Mom. I wanted to make you proud. We didn't win, but that's okay. We have lots of heart, but other teams had more time to train. There are a lot of other competitions left."

Mom put a finger under my chin and looked right in my eyes. "You stuck up for your friend. You made difficult choices, and you did the right thing. Like you always do. You make me prouder than you can

even imagine!" She softly hummed the song we'd sung. "You're the best daughter and the best big sister a family could have."

"Thanks, Mom," I said, giving her the biggest hug I could.

"I love you, Cora," she said.

As we swam away, I couldn't stop smiling.

Legend of Mermaids

These creatures of the sea have many secrets. Although people have believed in mermaids for centuries, nobody has ever proven their existence. People all over the world are attracted to the mysterious mermaids.

The earliest mermaid story dates back to around 1000 BC in an Assyrian legend. A goddess loved a human man but killed him accidentally. She fled to the water in shame. She tried to change into a fish, but the water would not let her hide her true nature. She lived the rest of her days as half-woman, half-fish.

Later, the ancient Greeks whispered tales of fishy women called sirens. These beautiful but deadly beings lured sailors to their graves. Many sailors feared or respected mermaids because of their association with doom.

Note: This text was taken from The Girl's Guide to Mermaids: Everything Alluring about These Mythical Beauties *by Sheri A. Johnson (Capstone Press, 2012). For more mermaid facts, be sure to check this book out!*

Talk It Out

1. Cora had always dreamed about being on the Spirit Squad. However, it didn't quite go how she thought it would. Talk about a time when your expectations had to change.

2. When Cora and Shyanna found out why Rachel didn't make the Spirit Squad, they were rightfully mad. Do you think they did the right thing when they talked to the Queen? What would you have done in the same situation?

3. Rachel didn't want her friends to find out how she really felt. Why is it important to talk about your feelings?

4. With three little sisters, Cora had a lot of extra responsibilities at home. Do you think it was fair that she had to help out so much? Defend your answer.

Write It Down

1. Pretend you are Cora. Make a pro and con list about leaving the Spirit Squad and starting a new one.

2. If Cora and Shyanna hadn't left the Spirit Squad for Rachel, do you think the three girls would still be friends? Write a few paragraphs explaining your reasons.

3. In this story, Regina was the mean girl/bully. Why do you think Regina acted that way? Write a few paragraphs from Regina's point of view. Be sure to include reasons for her actions, as they will help readers understand Regina better.

4. Write an alternate ending for the story. Maybe the two Spirit Squads from Neptunia tie and have to compete against each other. Maybe the two Spirit Squads form one big squad and compete together? It's your ending, so finish the story any way you want.

About the Author

Janet Gurtler has written numerous
well-received YA books. Mermaid Kingdom
is her debut series for younger readers. She
lives in Calgary, Alberta, near the Canadian
Rockies, with her husband, son, and a chubby
Chihuahua named Bruce. Gurtler does not
live in an igloo or play hockey, but she does
love maple syrup and says "eh" a lot.

About the Illustrator

Katie Wood fell in love with drawing
when she was very small. Since graduating
from Loughborough University School of
Art and Design in 2004, she has been living
her dream working as a freelance illustrator.
From her studio in Leicester, England, she
creates bright and lively illustrations for
books and magazines all over the world.

Dive in and get swept away!

Mermaid KINGDOM
by Janet Gurtler

Shyanna's Song

Mermaid KINGDOM
by Janet Gurtler

Rachel's Secret

Mermaid KINGDOM
by Janet Gurtler

Cora's Decision

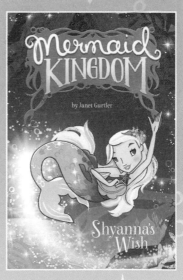

Mermaid KINGDOM
by Janet Gurtler

Shyanna's Wish